The Coffin Creaks

DAVID ORME

The Coffin Creaks
by David Orme
Illustrated by Jorge Mongiovi and Ulises Carpintero
Cover photograph: © manuel velasco

Published by Ransom Publishing Ltd.
Radley House, 8 St. Cross Road, Winchester, Hampshire, SO23 9HX, UK
www.ransom.co.uk

ISBN   978 184167 463 6

First published in 2011

Copyright © 2011 Ransom Publishing Ltd.

Illustrations copyright © 2011 Jorge Mongiovi and Ulises Carpintero

Printed in India by Imprint Digital Ltd.
Originally published in 1998 by Stanley Thornes Publishers Ltd.

A CIP catalogue record of this book is available from the British Library.

CONTENTS

NOT FOR THE PUBLIC TO KNOW
TOP SECRET
ZONE 13 FILES ONLY

4

THE BUILDING SITE

It had been a very boring day for Lorna.

Her school had closed for teacher's meetings. She had spent the whole day sitting in her dad's office. Looking out of the window, she could see him coming and going. They were building a new supermarket in the centre of town. Her dad was the site engineer.

'No, you can't stay at home by yourself,' Lorna's dad had said. 'Not after the trouble you got into last time.'

Lorna thought that was very unfair. The fire brigade had arrived in plenty of time to save the house. Anyway, she would rather burn to death than be bored to death in this office.

Lorna had brought her revision to do. There were exams next week, but it was difficult to think about her work. Outside, diggers trundled backwards and forwards.

She looked at her history book again. Why were the Tudors and Stuarts such a boring lot of people? Her teacher kept banging on about Henry the Eighth and what a great king he had been. Lorna thought he was a fat creep.

There was a yell from outside. She looked out of the window. The digger had stopped moving. It had sunk in the ground.

Another digger was brought up. It pulled out the sunken digger with a chain.

The men all gathered round, peering down into the hole. Lorna put down her history book. She wanted to look, too.

'What are you doing here? I told you to stay off the site! You haven't even got a hard hat on!'

That was typical of her dad. Why did he have to embarrass her in front of everybody?

One of the men came to her rescue. He plonked a hard hat on her head.

'Don't be too hard on her, boss!'

The ground had caved in under the weight of the digger. They could see the top of some steps going down into the dark.

'What do you reckon, boss?'

'Probably an old cellar. There have been buildings on this site for centuries. We'll fill it in tomorrow. It's not a problem. This will be the car park. We're not building here.'

A mysterious cellar, and all Dad wanted to do was fill it in! Lorna loved mysteries. Somehow, she was going to go down those steps.

NOT FOR THE PUBLIC TO KNOW

TOP SECRET

ZONE 13 FILES ONLY

DOWN THE STEPS

Lorna was allowed out that evening. She met up with Jason and Melissa. They were her two best friends. She told them what she had seen at the building site.

'I want to explore that cellar. There could be anything down there.'

Jason wasn't keen.

'It's a crazy idea. It could cave in and we might get trapped or crushed to death.'

Melissa thought it would be good to explore,
but she had a worry as well.

'How will we get to it? Isn't there a guard
dog and a security man?'

'They won't be a problem,' said Lorna. 'The
security man has a job during the day, so he
sleeps all night in the office. The guard dog
knows me. Anyway, he's as tame as anything.
They couldn't afford to get a fierce one.'

Soon the three friends were creeping through a hole in the fence. Dave, the guard dog, came running up, wagging his tail. He wanted to play, but Lorna sent him away.

They found the steps. Lorna had brought her father's powerful torch, and some spare batteries. She shone the light down.

Jason decided that, as he was male, he should go first. The girls didn't argue. They just pushed him out of the way.

The steps went down a short way, then ended up in a tiny room. The floor was thick with dust. Jason stamped on the floor.

'It sounds hollow under here.'

Stamping on the floor was a big mistake. They felt it collapsing under them. They were falling, sliding, down and down.

Lorna felt herself land with a thud on a pile of soft earth and rotten wood. Melissa landed on top of her. Jason thudded down next.

'Get off me!' Lorna yelled. She scrambled up. The torch was still working.

It was shining on an ancient wooden coffin. The side had fallen away. A skull was looking out at them.

The skull did not look pleased to see them.

NOT FOR THE PUBLIC TO KNOW
TOP SECRET
ZONE 13 FILES ONLY

IN THE CRYPT

They all screamed.

'We're in someone's grave!' wailed Melissa. 'I want to get out of here!'

'More than one person's grave,' said Lorna, in a shaky voice. 'Look!'

She shone the torch around. They were in a tunnel that stretched away into darkness. There were shelves along the wall. Coffins were stacked on the shelves. Some of the

coffins had rotted away, leaving piles of bones.

'There must have been an old church here, years ago,' said Jason. 'They had places like this where they buried people. They called them crypts.'

'Thanks for the history lesson, Jason,' said
Lorna. 'I'll stick to the Tudors and Stuarts if
you don't mind.'

'Perhaps they are Tudors and Stuarts,' said
Melissa. 'That might be Anne Boleyn over
there.'

'Don't be stupid,' said Jason. 'That one's still got a head. Anne Boleyn had hers chopped off.'

'Shut up, you two,' said Lorna. 'Let's just get out of here.'

That seemed easy, but it wasn't. They had fallen quite a long way. They could see the steps above them. How could they reach them now?

Melissa was the lightest. Jason lifted her up. She just got her fingertips onto the lowest step. She tried to pull herself up, but the whole step fell down. It just missed Lorna and Jason. It smashed into a rotting coffin, sending wood and bones and dust everywhere.

'Let's try shouting,' said Melissa. 'We might wake up the security guard.'

They all yelled and yelled. Their shouts echoed up and down the gloomy passage. If

any of the bodies in the coffins had wanted to rest in peace, there was no chance that night.

But Jeff, the security guard, slept on. Dave the guard dog heard them, but it sounded like trouble to him. He liked to keep out of trouble, so he stayed well away.

No Escape

'Let's head along the tunnel. There might be another way out,' said Lorna.

Jason and Melissa didn't think that was very likely. The crypt must have been sealed up and forgotten years and years ago.

'Why should anyone want to come here?' said Jason. 'I can't see people just popping in to see how great-aunt Mabel is getting on now that she's dead.'

No one liked the idea of a walk along the passage between the stacked coffins.

Melissa was terrified of treading on something crunchy. Jason was just terrified. He blamed Lorna for the mess they were in.

'You and your secret stairs! I told you it was dangerous, didn't I?'

Melissa joined in.

'You and your exploring! You're just like a kid!'

Lorna got cross. She decided to get her own back by turning off her torch.

There was total darkness.

Jason yelled in panic.

Melissa trod on something crunchy.

Lorna put the light back on. 'Now, shut up, or I'll do it again.'

It didn't take them long to reach the end of the tunnel. There, in the brick wall, was a door! Maybe they could get out after all.

Lorna shone the torch up and down it. On the floor in front of it was a pile of bones.

It was an awful sight. This skull wasn't clean and white, like the one in the science lab at school. It was a dirty brown, and had patches of dry skin on it. There were tufts of hair still sticking out of it.

'That one must have got fed up lying in its coffin and decided to go for a walk,' said Jason.

Melissa thought of something worse.

'Maybe that person wasn't really dead when they put him in here. Maybe he managed to get out of his coffin. Maybe he starved to death trying to open that door ...'

NOT FOR THE PUBLIC TO KNOW
TOP SECRET
ZONE 13 FILES ONLY

5

GOOD NEWS
- RATS!

That idea really cheered them up, especially
when they found that the door couldn't be
moved. They decided the best thing was to
wait until the morning, then try some more
yelling. Lorna remembered what her dad had
said. They were going to fill in the hole in the
morning. She decided not to tell the others
about that.

Jason took one last look at the door.

'Hey, point your light down there,' he said.

Lorna shone the light down towards the floor. There was a round hole at the bottom of the door.

'Good news!' said Jason. 'Rats!'

'If that's your idea of good news ...'

Jason explained.

'If rats can get in here, there must be a way through.'

'And we'll all squeeze through that little hole and pop off home, then.'

They tried kicking at the door again, but it wouldn't budge. They walked back down the passage to the place where they had fallen in. Lorna shone the torch the other way. They could see where the passage ended in a brick wall.

They sat down on the pile of soil that had fallen through with them. They knew they would have to stay there for the rest of the night.

Melissa was getting really upset. 'I don't want to go to sleep here,' she sobbed.

'You could stretch out on one of those shelves,' suggested Jason. 'They're just about your size.'

Jason wondered why Melissa hit him.

They sat for a while in silence. Lorna was really worried now. What if they fell asleep, and the digger started to fill in the hole before they woke up?

Then they heard the noises!

NOT FOR THE PUBLIC TO KNOW

TOP SECRET

ZONE 13 FILES ONLY

WHAT CAME OUT OF THE COFFIN

First, a faint scurrying sound started at the end of the passage.

'Told you!' said Jason. 'Rats!'

Any minute, they expected to feel furry bodies running over their feet. There can't be much left to eat on these dry bones, thought Lorna. She wondered what it would be like to be eaten alive by hundreds of rats.

She jumped up.

'Shout, make a noise. It might frighten them away.'

They all yelled and screamed, and it seemed to do the trick. The scurrying sound stopped. The rats must have been surprised. The people in the crypt weren't usually this noisy.

Then they heard a scratching, creaking noise.

Lorna shone the torch. The sound was coming from one of the coffins.

They clutched each other. Lorna remembered a horror film she had once seen. Any minute she expected the lid to creak open.

'Perhaps he just wants us to keep the noise down.'

'Shut up, Jason,' hissed Melissa.

They watched the coffin in horror. The sides were giving way, the heavy lid was sinking ...

A piece of wood fell away. Immediately, hundreds of large, black beetles tumbled out

of the coffin. They heard the sound of their scratchy feet. Lorna felt one crawling up her leg.

Then they heard the voice. It echoed and boomed around the crypt.

'What are you doing here ... ?'

JEFF WAKES UP

How were they to know it was Jeff, the security guard?

He didn't sleep all through the night. Every couple of hours, his alarm clock woke him up and he had a quick walk round.

He heard the screams. When he shone his light down the hole, he saw Lorna and the others leaping about in a crypt full of rotting coffins. It came as quite a surprise.

He managed to push a ladder down and the three friends climbed out.

They were filthy and still very frightened. The security guard knew Lorna.

'Right, over to the office. I'm calling your dad. You're in real trouble now.'

'Would that be the office where you've been asleep for the last two hours?' asked Lorna.

That made him think a bit. Being a security guard was a cushy job. He didn't want to lose it.

'Get out of here, and don't come back!'

000//000

When Lorna got home, her dad was waiting for her.

'You're late. And look at the state you're in! What have you been doing?'

'I've been studying history, Dad.'

'What history?'

'Well, they might have been Tudors and Stuarts.'